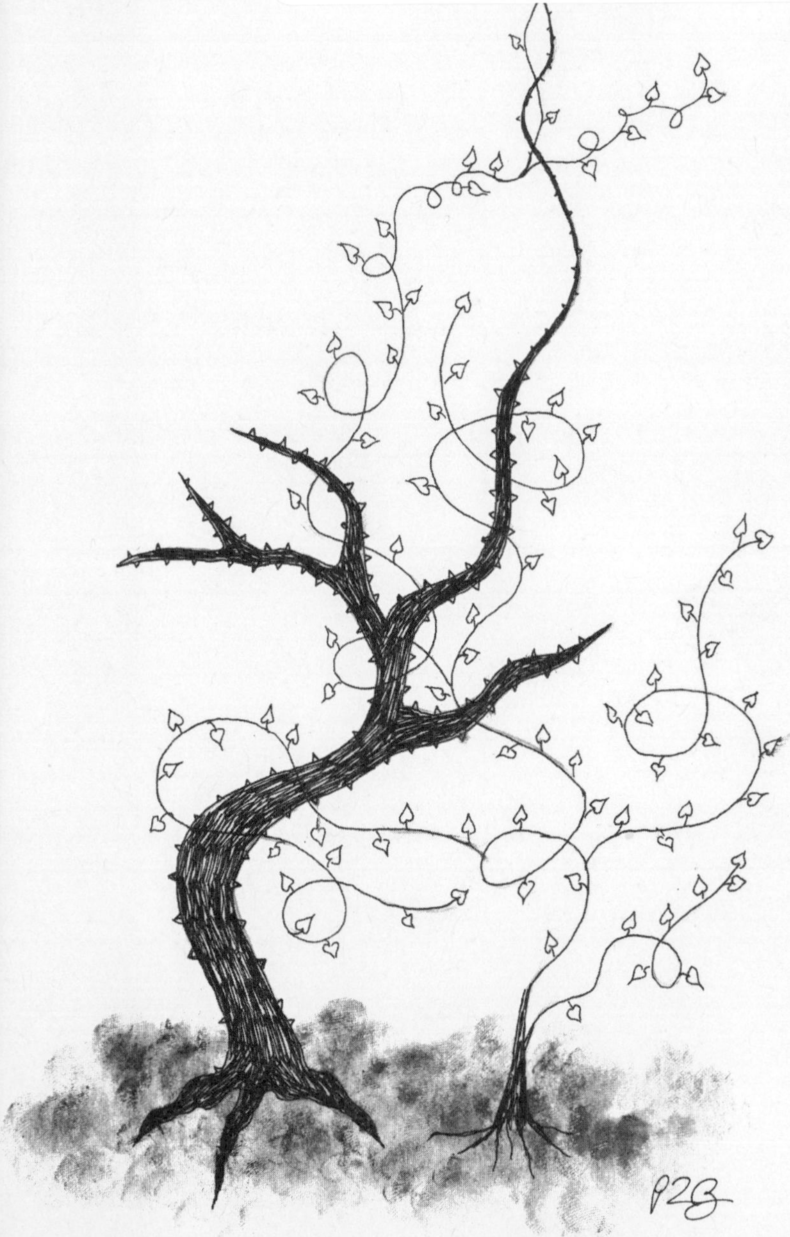

This special signed edition is limited to
600 numbered copies and 9 lettered copies.

This is copy 429.

Plastic Jesus

Plastic Jesus

Poppy Z. Brite

Subterranean Press ✳ 2000

Plastic Jesus
Copyright © 2000 by Poppy Z. Brite. All rights reserved.

Dustjacket Copyright © 2000 by Mary Fleener.
All rights reserved.

Interior illustrations Copyright © 2000 by Poppy Z. Brite.
All rights reserved.

Interior design Copyright © 2000 by Tim Holt.
All rights reserved.

Limited Edition
(ISBN 1-892284-64-2)
May 2000

Trade Edition
(ISBN 1-892284-65-0)
September 2000

Subterranean Press
P.O. Box 190106
Burton, MI 48519

email:
publisher@subterraneanpress.com

website:
www.subterraneanpress.com

Plastic Jesus

i

Seth Grealy's knees buckled and he went down like a house of cards as five bullets tore into him.

What had come out of the cold New York night to inflict this pain? He didn't know, hadn't seen it coming at all though a part of him had expected it for most of his forty-five years. He'd thought it would happen onstage, though, something well-aimed and high-caliber if he was lucky. Not right here outside his building, almost home.

He knew he'd been shot, had heard each pop separately and clearly, a long pause between the third and the final two, as he spun and hit the sidewalk. Had felt the bullets enter his back, his throat. Wasn't the body supposed to go into shock, to start churning out its own natural painkillers? Maybe he'd fucked up his system with all the artificial ones over the years, for the pain was voracious, unforgiving.

The doorman was kneeling over him now, red-coated arms spread wide, protecting him from curious passersby. Where was Peyton? He'd thought his partner was right behind him as he got out of the limo.

"Oh my God, it's Seth Grealy!" a woman screamed. "They've shot Seth Grealy!"

Seth rolled his head a little to the side, perceived the woman as a large colorful shape squatting nearby, doing something to the sidewalk— what?—soaking a scrap of paper in the spreading pool of his blood. The doorman made a grab for her, but the woman was off with her priceless souvenir. *Like Dillinger,* Seth thought dazedly, not sure if that was right.

"Mr. Grealy, Mr. Grealy, can you hear me? The ambulance is coming."

"I think it may as well take its time," he wanted to say, but what came out was little more than a wet gasp. He felt blood gobbing from his mouth, cascading down his chin. For the first time since he'd hit the sidewalk, Seth Grealy considered the possibility that he was about to die.

Why did the thought make him feel sunlight on his face? There was no sunlight here, only the winter night, the cold wind sweeping off the park, the huge, paralyzing pain.

The ambulance cut its siren as it turned onto the block, but left its red bubbles revolving, wash-

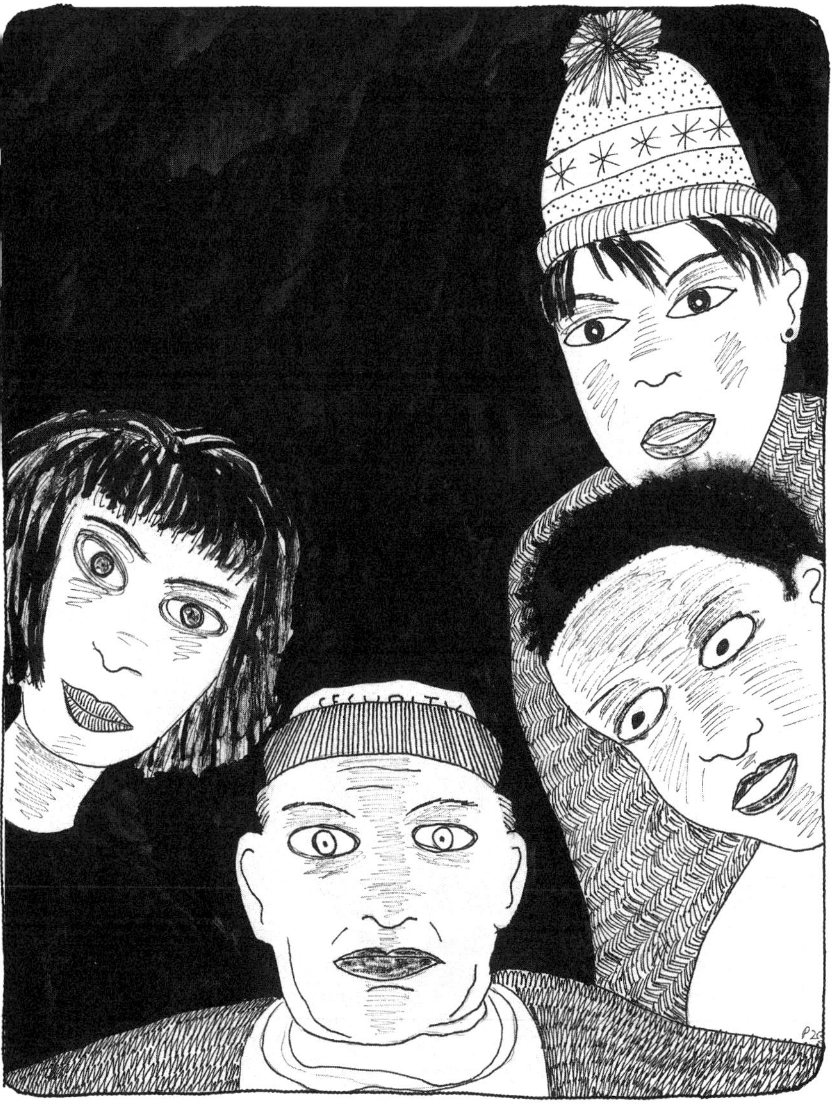

ing the faces of the crowd, the black puddle on the sidewalk, the stone façade of the apartment building with a bloody light. The paramedics descended upon him, and Seth could have sworn he saw one of them shake her head—*This one's not gonna make it*—before they hoisted him into the back of the ambulance.

"Shot the fuck out of him, hunh?" said somebody waiting in the back.

"Shut up, man, I think he's still conscious—"

The medic who'd spoken first was fitting a plastic mask over Seth's nose and mouth. "Shit, this ain't doin' any good, the oxygen's just comin' out those holes in his throat."

The woman medic's voice rose. "I said he might still be *conscious,* Washington!"

Washington's eyes crinkled in disbelief, then sought Seth's. "Mr. Grealy? Can you hear me? Do you know who you are?"

He thought he managed a little nod, but Washington didn't get it. The big face loomed closer. "DO YOU KNOW WHO YOU ARE?"

A philosophical approach was called for, then; had he ever? Through all the money and drugs, through all the women and men, at the heights of his art and the depths of his insane fame, even with Peyton, had he ever known who he was?

The implications of this question seemed vast, and Seth let himself drift on them until he felt the sunlight touching his face again.

ii

Peyton had done all the things required of him, save one. He'd gone to the hospital and ridden down in the gleaming metal elevator to the morgue to perform the wholly unnecessary task of identifying Seth's body. Anyone in the world could have identified Seth's body, he thought, but that wasn't the point. He had to be here, and here he was, breathing the formaldehyde smell that stung his nostrils, that masked something sweeter and darker. And here, rolled out on a table of more gleaming steel, was Seth.

He went right to the edge of the table, looked down into Seth's face. The lips were drawn tightly across the teeth in a grimace of surprise or pain, or perhaps only a reflex of rigor mortis. The eyes were closed, the lids slack. Only with his eyes closed had Seth ever looked at peace. He didn't look at peace now.

"All right, old man," said Peyton. "It'll be all right." He touched Seth's cheek. It was cold and tacky with blood. Seth's jacket and shirt had been cut or torn off in the efforts to stop the bleeding, which must have been like trying to stem the flow of Niagara Falls. His arms hung oddly in their sockets. His chest was covered with a layer of half-dried arterial blood like red stained glass. The entry wounds made by the bullets were small, dark, not so terrible. Peyton couldn't see any of the exit wounds.

"Could I have a towel, please?" he asked one of the morgue attendants.

"Sir?"

"A towel. And some water. I want to wash the blood off of him."

"You don't have to do that, sir, we can—"

"I want to do it."

Something in his tone must have convinced the attendant he was serious, or maybe morgue people were just used to dealing with the half-crazy bereaved. At any rate, Peyton was brought a towel and a basin of warm water, and they left him alone while he washed the blood from Seth's face and chest. While he took a comb from his own pocket and combed as much of it as possible out of Seth's hair. While he stood for a long time beside the metal table, one hand gripping its edge very tightly, the other entwined in Seth's stiffening fingers.

He stayed at the hospital all night. He could

not bear to go home yet, could not bear the throngs that would have gathered now outside the apartment building, carrying flowers, crying, singing Seth's songs. The very force of their sympathy might kill him. He rode the next morning in the hearse to Long Island, Seth in a plain casket in the back, and sat in the waiting salon of the crematorium for a few hours. Only then, with the white cardboard box of ashes like an eternal weight on his lap, did Peyton return to the home he had shared with Seth.

He took phone calls, took pills, slept a lot. He learned what he could of the killer, Ray Brinker. The man was described by the media as a fundamentalist Christian who deplored the political and social changes Seth had wrought in the world. He invoked the specter of AIDS as God's punishment upon homosexuals, and suggested that Seth had been a vector for the disease. His most-quoted public statement to date was, "I wish I could have killed him before he got this far."

Peyton allotted himself a certain amount of time to regain the poise he would need for the last thing he had to do. When he had reached that point, he called the man he believed could help him.

Dr. Jonathan Pumphrey was the embodiment of WASPiness, if a slightly effete version thereof.

His suits, always perfectly pressed, were Paul Stuart, his briefcase Mark Cross. Once, egged on by his boyfriend Rick, he had bought a black Valentino suit, but he never wore it. His blonde hair, undarkened since childhood, parted on the left and fell engagingly over his forehead. He did not mind at all that he stood only five-foot-nine in his glossy Gucci loafers, for he felt that being small and neat was infinitely preferable to being big and sloppy.

He'd always thought of Seth Grealy as big and sloppy, even though the man really hadn't been. Seth was quite tall, even rather shambling, but he always looked clean. It was his presence that was big and sloppy; it sloshed everywhere, got all over everything, made him seem larger than he was. Jonathan had heard that very famous people often had such an exaggerated presence, but until today, Seth Grealy was the only mega-celebrity he'd ever met. Now he was about to meet another: Peyton Masters, Seth's bereaved musical partner and lover, was in his waiting room.

Seth Grealy had visited Jonathan's midtown office twice a week for five years until his death a fortnight ago. Except for brief *incommunicado* periods, he never missed a session. Jonathan was Seth Grealy's psychiatrist, more commonly referred to by Seth as his head-shrinker, his witch doctor, or his little tin Freud, depending upon how bad Seth's mood was on any given day.

Jonathan often wondered whether Seth would

have gone into therapy with him had the man known to what extent he had been Jonathan's teenage idol. Jonathan was ten years younger than Seth, and had seen the famous Stonewall interview with Seth and Peyton when he was still a teenager agonizing over his sexuality. Without it, without *them,* he believed he might still be living in the closet.

But Seth Grealy had had no idea that a young and confused Jonathan Pumphrey had once owned all his records, hung posters of him on the wall and occasionally even masturbated to those posters. He didn't know he had been a shaping force in Jonathan's life. He'd just wanted a therapist who wasn't "an old fart," as he put it, and he'd been given Jonathan's number by a friendly GP who knew Jonathan was fresh out of medical school with a hungry new practice, and he'd called to set up an appointment. That was where they had begun.

Though Jonathan had counseled many patients for grief, he couldn't imagine how he would survive if Rick died. He wondered how Peyton was managing to get along without Seth. He felt he had come to know Peyton Masters vicariously through Seth's therapy, and suspected there was a core of steel in the man that could survive just about any loss. But mustn't it be different if, in addition to suddenly, brutally losing your lover, you also found yourself now only half of a world-beloved gestalt? Mustn't it cleave you too, somehow?

Jonathan thought of the picture they had presented to the world, Peyton's sweetness and Seth's studied bad-boy act. You could tie your mind in psychedelic knots with Seth's songs, then clear your head with Peyton's. To the world they were equals: equal in genius, equal in love. But Jonathan knew how dependent Seth had become on Peyton in the past decade. He felt sure that Seth could not have survived Peyton's death. He wondered whether Peyton was experiencing survivor's guilt, especially since he'd been right behind Seth when the murder took place.

The news had come shockingly to Jonathan two weeks ago, the morning after Seth was killed, Rick calling the office and saying in a shaken voice, "Turn on the news, baby, it's Seth Grealy." Jonathan canceled his sessions, sat by the radio all day, tried to take it in. Apparently Peyton had remained in the limo during the shooting and its immediate aftermath. Seth had just unfolded his lanky frame from the car and Peyton was sliding across the seat to get out when the shots began. In a bit of quick thinking that may have saved Peyton Masters' life, the driver twisted around, grabbed a handful of his heavy winter coat, and hauled him back into the limo. By the time he fought his way out, the doorman of the building had gotten the gun away from Brinker and Seth was beyond recognizing anybody. How did one stand such a thing?

Jonathan took a peek in the mirror, smoothed his hair over his forehead, straightened his tie. He went to the door of his office, hesitated for a moment, then opened it. "Please come in, Mr. Masters."

As Peyton stood, Jonathan experienced a moment of the dissonance that is often involved when confronted with the real-life version of a famous face. Peyton had always been stereotyped as the "cutest" of the Kydds, with his charismatic curly smile, thick dark shock of hair, and liquid long-lashed eyes. Seth and Peyton had been out of the public eye for some time, so Jonathan's mental image of Peyton was several years out of date. Still, the majority of the changes appeared recent: the red-rimmed eyes; a few days' worth of beard stubble; a look of hollowness.

"First off, Dr. Pumphrey, please call me Peyton."

"Of course. Peyton, I said it when we spoke on the phone but I want to say again, I'm so sorry for what happened—"

Peyton waved it aside. The gesture seemed not so much rude as weary. "Thanks, yes, of course you are. Everyone's sorry, and they all tell me so, and oddly enough none of it helps."

Peyton had lost far more of his Leyborough accent than Seth ever had. Nothing else about Seth was working-class by the time he died, but he had kept that guttural accent, born for cursing and trained for singing.

At Jonathan's invitation, Peyton folded himself into a big leather chair. He was taller than Jonathan, but in the chair—or perhaps just diminished by his sorrow—he appeared small. "I'm not sure why I wanted to see you, Dr. Pumphrey. I suppose it's because you were the only other person Seth spent much time talking to. He'd lost faith in people. Well, he never had much to begin with, but he'd gotten disillusioned. Said people credited us with changing the world, and so thought they didn't need to do anything for themselves. I'd say, well, we *did* change the world, and he'd say it was true but not true enough. Said a thing like AIDS wouldn't have been allowed to happen if we'd really changed it. Didn't want to see any of our old friends or make any new ones. Said we hadn't needed anyone else when we met, back when it was just us two, and we didn't need anyone now. He said a lot of nonsense, actually. I'm sure you've heard all this already."

"I know a great deal about Seth's recent years," Jonathan allowed. "I never really knew much about how you met. Other than the public stuff, of course."

"Seth never told you?"

"We hadn't gotten that far yet. Between working through his childhood and dealing with his more recent crises—the heroin addiction, for example—"

"You know how he finally kicked it?"

"Yes." Jonathan took a pressed linen handkerchief from his breast pocket, touched his lips in an unconscious gesture of distaste, and tucked it neatly away again. "You chartered a plane..."

"A private jet. Very plush, very comfortable. Seth had everything he needed, except the smack. We stopped in Tokyo and the Seychelles for fuel. Twice around the world altogether, till he was clean."

"But it made him very ill?"

"Oh, Christ, yes—wallowing in his own spew and begging me to inject him with smack or cut his throat, he didn't care which. When I couldn't stand it, I'd go up front and work on a song I was writing for him. That turned out to be 'Without You.'"

It was a slow, beautiful song. Jonathan thought of the lyrics:

Everything you do just leaves me speechless
You're the strongest and most graceful thing I know
You've said I give you melody
But without you I would be
Nothing but a lot of show...

He hadn't known Peyton wrote the song for Seth, certainly wouldn't have guessed the circumstances, but it made sense.

"It was just typical Grealy melodrama," Peyton went on. "Certainly he was hurting, but he was milking it, too. I lived with various Grealy melodramas for twenty-two years. Never saw one I couldn't get through."

There was a long, uncomfortable pause.

"Except this last one," Peyton said finally. "Seth always said I had a tendency to state the obvious. Musically and otherwise. Said he could see it right from the start."

"I know he could be harsh."

"Oh, most of it rolled right off my back. Seth abused people when he was unsure of himself. He was full of bluster when we first met, and he never lost it."

Full of bluster. That was exactly how Seth had been, and the phrase undammed something within Jonathan. He thought he'd done his grieving, but apparently he hadn't. He missed his patient; he missed his idol; but most of all he missed the remarkable man he'd been privileged to know for a little while.

"I'd like to know more about how you met," Jonathan said. It was the only thing he could think of, because he was suddenly afraid he might cry.

"Right, I suppose it might do me some good to talk about it. You'll forgive me if I get, well, emotional."

"I'll forgive you if you'll forgive me."

And Peyton began to tell the story.

iii

A spring night in the late nineteen-fifties, in the blighted green landscape of industrial northern England: Leyborough. The war was nearly twenty years past, but parts of this city still stood in blackened ruins, reminders of fire and death from the sky. Pensioners here still hoarded their tinned goods, and the outskirts had become studded with council estates, warrens where the poor were packed in like the inhabitants of some Calcutta slum.

Seventeen-year-old Seth Grealy, neither rich nor poor, sprawled on his bed plucking idly at the strings of his guitar. His fingers were calloused from the learning, his nails splintered with it. His hair was combed carefully back from his forehead, plastered there with enough grease to leave stains on his pillowcase, and he'd grown his sideburns long. If anyone except his grandmother asked him, Seth said the hairstyle was meant to look like a duck's arse. Couldn't talk that way to Gran, could he; she lived a few miles down the road and they seldom saw her, but she paid his and Dad's bills. As soon as Seth was out of school she wanted him to get a job. Sign on at the munitions factory, or maybe one of the big cargo ships that had once been Leyborough's lifeblood. The thought of the sea brought him a vague sick horror. All that endless humping water, no escape.

As far as Seth was concerned, school couldn't be over soon enough, but he didn't want any fucking job. He wanted a band, and today he thought he had come closer to getting one. He choked up on the neck of the guitar, wondering how someone like Carl Perkins could make the instrument scream, whether he'd ever be able to create such a sound himself, and how in the world little Peyton Masters managed to tune the bloody thing by ear.

They'd met this day, Seth and Peyton, introduced at a mutual friend's house while sagging off school, both carrying £12 acoustic guitars they'd gotten for Christmas. It was great to meet someone else interested in American rock and roll—Peyton knew all the lyrics to Elvis Presley's "Hound Dog." Still, Seth hadn't expected this wide-eyed fifteen-year-old to actually know his way around on the guitar. But Peyton sat there with a little smile on his face and played it better than Seth, in fact better than anyone Seth knew personally.

Plastic Jesus

There had been something else, too. Seth had always had a lot of friends, neighborhood boys and mates from school. But there was no best friend, not even a close friend, never really had been. He slept with girls who were willing but had not been truly intimate with any of them. He supposed it had something to do with losing his mum. Freud would think so, the dirty old bastard. Everything always went back to Mummy. But something in the way he and Peyton had communicated so effortlessly today, both in words and through their guitars, made Seth think Peyton was different.

He was probably just going soft. He put down the guitar, picked up a notebook and pen, looked at them for a minute and tossed them back down.

All the surfaces and corners of Seth's narrow bedroom were piled with books, notebooks, sketchbooks, and various scraps of paper. For fourteen of his seventeen years—ever since his mother had taught him to read and write at age three—Seth had lived much of his life on paper. He wrote stories and made drawings for Mum. Made her smile, made her say she was proud.

Later, when she was going through what he and Dad thought was a difficult pregnancy, Seth sat beside her bed and read aloud to her. He was twelve. They'd gotten through most of *Great Expectations* before the doctor discovered that there was no baby growing inside her after all. An operation took place too late; Rosemary Grealy bled to death on the operating table before they had finished removing the fist of malignant flesh from her womb.

Though the door was closed, Seth could still smell the greasy smoke from the pan of chips his dad had burned earlier. Dad was gone now, almost certainly down to the pub, that was if he hadn't toppled into a ditch on the way. Seth smirked at the thought of his father's legs thrashing. No such luck, though. God looks after drunks and fools, and damned if old Oliver Grealy didn't qualify on both counts.

Usually the smell of chips, even his dad's burnt ones, made Seth hungry. Tonight he didn't have room for food. The leftover energy from the meeting turned him restless, wishing to do a hundred things but unable to concentrate on any. He'd gotten Peyton's number and wanted to ring him, but that would make Seth look queer as well as soft. He sometimes wondered if he might be a bit queer; the way he felt when he saw a picture of Elvis or James Dean wasn't the same as when he looked at a beautiful girl, but there was something sexual about it nonetheless. Something raw.

He wasn't queer for Peyton, though. Theirs was a meeting of minds. Minds and guitars: the two things Seth was betting on to get him out of Leyborough and into a real life.

Peyton, upon their meeting, did not experience the twinge of sexual confusion that Seth did: his heterosexuality was so unambiguous that he'd never even given it a thought. He was clear-skinned and dark-eyed, girls liked him, and he accepted that with an uncomplicated enjoyment.

He was thrilled, though, for he too had sensed the possibility of a real partnership. He knew other boys at school who listened to American rock and roll, but nobody who knew the flesh and the lonesome bones of it as Seth did. Upon arriving home, he dashed around the house to annoy his parents and sisters, telling them again and again, "I've met a kid who knows more about music than I do, and we're going to have a band!" Even though Seth had said nothing today about forming a band, Peyton repeated this as if it were the gospel truth. As far as he was concerned, it was.

The family had heard plans for Peyton's bands before; they were only surprised at the admission that someone he'd just met knew more than he did. Peyton had always been a good-natured, polite boy, but his sisters often accused him of believing he was smarter than anyone else in Leyborough, and Peyton never denied it.

Finally, he went to his room and sat up late with his guitar, teaching himself a whole new chord that night. He knew he was good, but he had to get a lot better: for Seth, for the band. Seth only wanted out of Leyborough; he'd said as much. Peyton wanted everything.

The following week, Seth reckoned enough time had gone by that he could ring Peyton without looking soft or queer. They met at Peyton's house the next day. Peyton answered the door holding his guitar. Seth's own was strapped across his back. It would not be quite proper to say they went to Peyton's bedroom like a pair of newlyweds approaching their honeymoon chamber, for they did not even know they were married yet. Later, though, they would both make the comparison.

They felt their way through a number of songs they both knew, just getting each other's rhythm: "Hound Dog," "Maybellene," "Twenty Flight Rock." Then Seth played one he'd written himself. The words were mostly a lot of nonsense, but the tune, he thought, had a certain snarl to it.

"That's really good," said Peyton. "You know, though, I think the chorus could be a little tighter—"

"It's not supposed to be *tight*."

Peyton just smiled and started strumming again, a tune Seth didn't recognize at first. Then he realized it was the one he'd just played, run through Peyton's filter. Later, the same thing would drive him to rage, but this first time he felt only fascination. To have someone—another musician—play his music back to him with a twist was weirdly intoxicating.

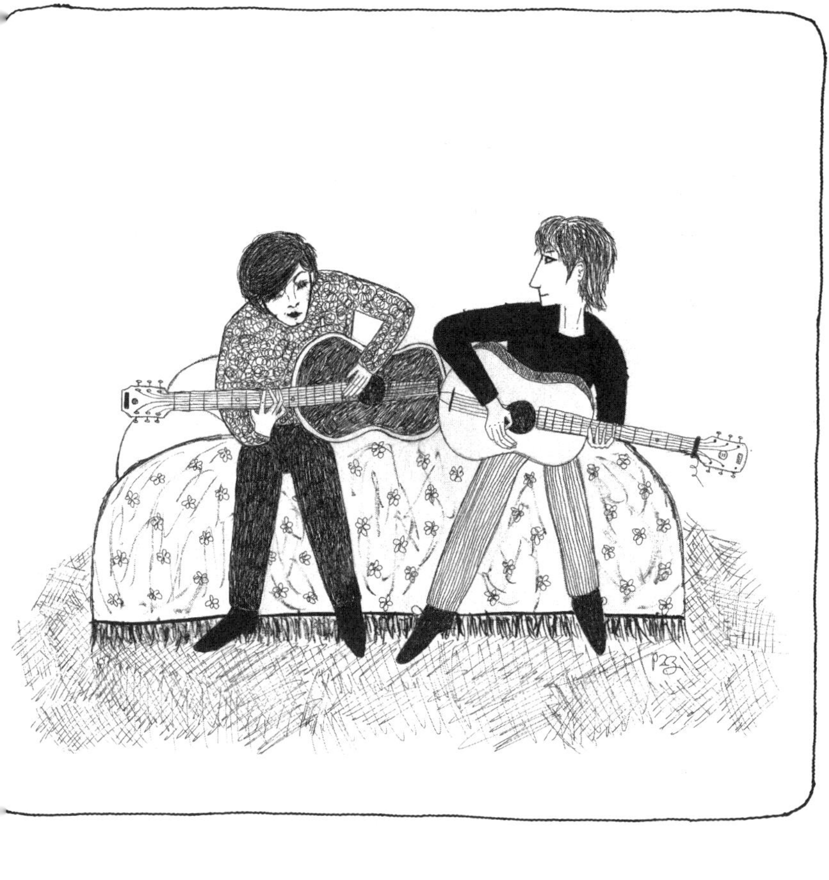

"Huh," said Seth by way of acknowledgment. "Not bad. Written anything yourself?"

"Oh, yeah, lots of stuff. Listen to this." He began another song in a chord Seth didn't even know. The lyrics weren't any better than Seth's, but it was beginning to dawn on Seth that this kid couldn't just play guitar, he could sing too. And their voices sounded good together. Maybe they could figure out some kind of harmony thing, something like the black girl groups did.

They played for hours, until their fingertips were reddened and grooved, until their throats were hoarse. Then they agreed to do it again the next day. When Seth had gone, Peyton sat at the old upright piano in his parents' parlor and played one last song, not a rock tune but one that summed up his feelings perfectly: "It's Almost Like Being in Love."

iv

There was a musical revolution afoot in Leyborough in 1961. The problem was, Harold Loomis was the only man who knew it existed.

He'd seen the band play two weeks ago at a club called Blaggers, a filthy back room full of teenagers drunk on cheap ale and nascent rock and roll. They had heard the music of Elvis Presley, Chuck Berry, Little Richard; it made them feel isolated, hemmed in by the sea and the times. Now they were hearing similar music on their own soil, played by boys they'd grown up with. The atmosphere in the club was simmering, truculent yet elated, and most definitely drenched in hormones. Harold had listened to half the set and gone home early. But he knew the band was something special.

Apparently they'd been playing together for about a year. Harold heard of them through a friend, who in turn had heard of them from some piece of rough trade he'd picked up in Yardley Park. "They're fuckin' brilliant," the boy had supposedly said. "Every kid I know is talkin' about them. If they was to put out a record, it'd sell a hundred fuckin' copies."

The idea of selling a hundred copies did not impress Harold—he had worked in his father's record store for years—but the idea that the youth of Leyborough was talking about this band interested him tremendously. He was twenty-seven, but he tried to keep up with the kids' taste in order to stock the store, and English music had been out of vogue for some time now. They wanted American rock and roll music. If a hometown band had captivated them, Harold wanted to know about it.

Most likely, he'd expected, they would simply be copying the American stuff. But they weren't. They had obviously been influenced by it, probably would not have existed without it, but they already had their own voice. The singer and lead guitarist, Seth Grealy, was a twenty-one-year-old firebrand: long and lean, with hair the color of rust and sly Satanic eyes. The second guitarist, Peyton Masters, was nineteen but looked closer to sixteen; with his fuck-me eyes and angelic harmonies, he could have been the schoolboy in a dirty old man's fantasies. (*Not* his own fantasies, Harold reminded himself; his interest in these boys was entirely professional). The rhythm section were nothing special, apparently a couple of Grealy's ne'er-do-well friends, but no matter. That was only one of the many things with which Harold could assist them.

He became absorbed in ideas of management, riches, world travels. So captivated was he by his fantasies that it took him two weeks to actually contact the band.

"Sethy? Man wants to see you out front. Bit of a posh type, you know, wearing a suit? Says he, eh, *manages records*."

Seth nodded thanks to Mark, his bass player, not letting the trace of excitement he felt show in his face. Mark was even younger than Peyton, and no matter how much Seth believed in this band, he couldn't allow these kids to get their hopes up falsely. He ducked his head to clear the low frame of the backstage door. If the front of Blaggers was a filthy hole, the back of the place was positively cavelike. Ducking dislodged the James Dean-style cap he wore, and as he came around the stage, it slid off his head. He was about to bend and pick it up when a man did so for him.

Seth was transfixed by the sight of this slight, well-pressed, altogether normal-looking man stooping to pick up his greasy black leather cap, actually brushing off the grime from the floor before handing it back to Seth with a slight nod. Seth nodded back, his eyes wary as he readjusted the cap on his head. No man had ever knelt before him.

"Seth Grealy? I'm Harold Loomis. My family owns Loomis Gramophones and Records, on Hill Street? You may know it—" Loomis paused as Seth burst out laughing.

"Sorry, sorry Mister Loomis, it's just Marky said you were a record manager and he must have thought you meant—well, and I guess I did too. Joke's on us, you see?"

"Perhaps not," Loomis said rather prissily. "I do manage a record store, but I also have connections with radio stations and with certain people in London. I can't make any promises, but I think at the very least I could help you record a demo tape."

Seth wasn't laughing anymore. His keen eyes studied this man, searching for any hint of fakery. "Why'd you come to me?" he asked. "We're a solid group, you know. We're together for the long haul."

"Well, it struck me that you were the *de facto* leader of the group. Being the front man and so forth. Also, I'd heard that you were calling yourselves, er, Seth and the Silver Dreams at one point, before you shortened it—"

"Don't think much of our name, do you, Mr. Loomis?" It was the way Loomis pronounced the band's name, not quite mockingly but with no

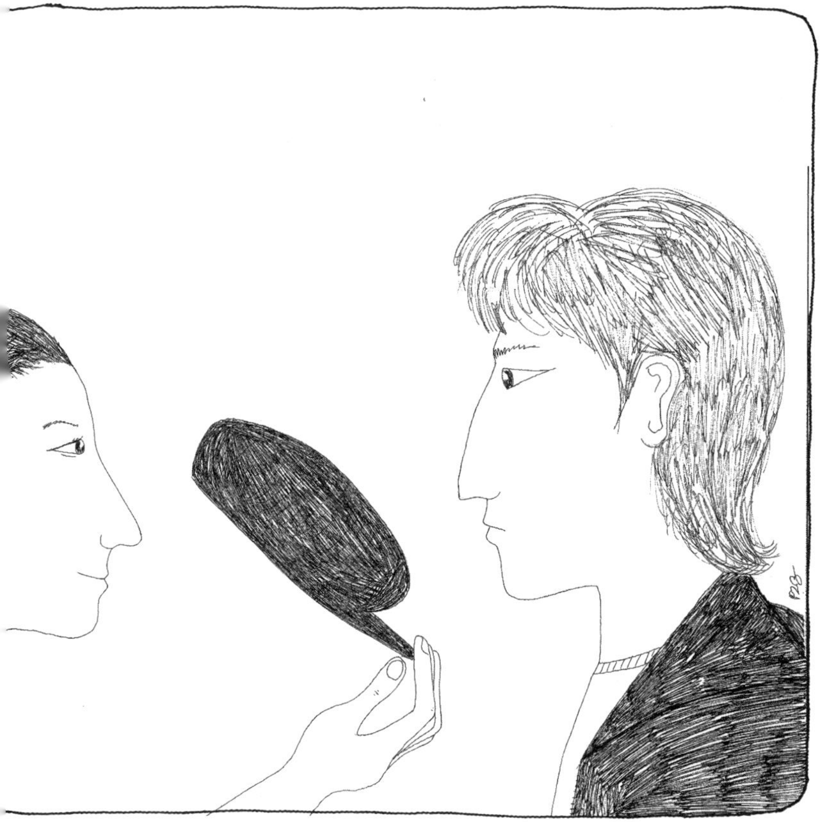

enthusiasm, that told Seth this. He'd wondered about it too; the name as much as anything else had to be perfect.

"It's Harold, please. And frankly, no, I don't. Really—the Silver Dreams? There are a hundred groups in England with names that sound the same, all trying to play American music better than the Americans. I think you're doing something more than that, and you should have a name to reflect it."

"Silver Dreams was Peyton's idea," said Seth. "I'm not married to it. I suppose you've got a better idea, *Harold?*"

"I think so."

"Let's hear it then."

"The Kydds," said Harold.

Seth blinked. "Kids?"

"K-Y-D-D-S. The unique spelling helps it to catch the eye, but the name itself is so very basic, so very rock and roll. Who buys rock records? The kids. Who can make you the biggest band in the world? The kids. This name shows that you're part of them."

"Part of who?" Peyton asked.

Both men turned. Peyton Masters stood in the shadows to the side of the stage, smiling slightly. Seth met his eyes and wondered how long he had been listening.

"Part of the Youth Revolution, Peyt. At least, this fellow reckons he can make us a part of it." It seemed important to bring Peyton into the conversation, to prove Seth hadn't been having some kind of clandestine head-to-head with Loomis. "He's a sort of record manager."

Peyton stepped forward and extended his hand. As the nineteen-year-old introduced himself and shook hands with the man, Seth had a sense that Peyton had suddenly grown older than his years. There was nothing of the innocent schoolboy to him just now. Instead there was a confident set to his jaw, a subtle squaring of his shoulders that made him look as though he knew all about managers, demos, and deals. It was at that moment, Seth reflected much later, that Peyton had shown Harold Loomis who was really the leader of the band.

V

Blaggers didn't even know enough to renew their contract as house band after a year. Harold Loomis wasn't worried. By that time the Kydds' name had been heard outside of Leyborough. Clubs in other cities wanted something fresh, a band that had made it big coming from a place where no band had a prayer of ever making it big. Their first single, Peyton's "Cry My Tears Away," backed with Seth's "Dig Your Man," climbed the English charts of 1963 like a carnival bell hit by a strongman's mallet.

"Cry My Tears Away" was the source of the first huge blowup between Peyton and Seth. They'd bickered amiably and not so amiably over the merits of various songs, sparred for the position of lead guitar, even once had a tussle that brought Peyton's mother to the bedroom door, knocking worriedly. That one had turned out to be about a particular Chuck Berry song they wanted to cover; Seth felt the vocals should be handled in a particular way, a way with which Peyton vehemently disagreed. There had also been a dust-up during which Dennis, their drummer, had had to pull them off each other—but everyone had been drunk that night. "Cry My Tears Away" was the first thing that nearly broke up the Kydds.

It was a pretty love song, a very pretty love song that would no doubt flutter the heartstrings of every little girl who heard it. It was catchy, almost *too* catchy, so that you'd find yourself humming it hours after you had vowed to put it out of your mind. (Harold told them there was a German phrase for this phenomenon, one that roughly translated as "earworm.") However—as Seth pointed out the first time Peyton played it for him, and never ceased to point out for the rest of his life—*it had no edge.*

Why should a band release as its first single a song that had no edge? What would prevent the Kydds from sinking traceless into the morass of sweet-ballad bands, bunches of nice boys who wrote love songs, damp-knicker bands as Seth derisively dubbed them? Why should they disappear before they'd even had a chance to start? Why not set out with an edge?

"Because *no one who hears my song ever forgets it!*" cried Peyton. They were in Harold's living room, where they could argue as loudly as they liked without parental interference. Harold lurked in the kitchenette, close enough both to eavesdrop and to keep an eye on his breakables. "No one will forget it once they've heard it on the *radio,* once they've bought the *single,* don't you see? And they won't forget us either, they'll buy the record and they'll listen to 'Dig Your Man,' it's a great, great song—"

"Fuck you." Seth made as if to walk out of the flat, but stopped when he saw that Peyton would not pursue him. *"Your* song is bloody unforgettable, *my* song's a nice addition to the record. How about, *my* song'll get us noticed because it doesn't sound just like a hundred others?"

"Neither does mine," said Peyton, "and you know it. It sounds a little like the hundred others, but there's a difference, and everyone will hear it, and buy it."

"Shit."

"You know I'm right."

"I'm going out for a bottle."

It went on like that for days, and they said things they regretted (or Peyton did—it's difficult to know if Seth was ever capable of regretting his own actions), but of course "Cry My Tears Away" made the A-side of the single. Even more significant, Seth and Peyton discovered a formula that would get them through the next twenty-odd years: a great blowout of a fight made them appreciate each other even more afterwards. There was no one else in either of their lives to whom they could say those sorts of things, and certainly no one who would forgive them for it, even thank them eventually—for it could not be denied that, through fighting and cajoling and sometimes pure coercion, they improved each other musically. They honed themselves on each other. The more they saw of the music business, the more they realized how rare such a partnership was.

So "Cry My Tears Away" ate up charts and radio time, and critics praised the raw, edgy power of the flip side, "Dig Your Man." The rhythm section made a perfect platform for the vocal harmonies: Peyton's voice all sweet turquoise velvet, Seth's reedy, woody, slightly hoarse, and the two woven together like a medieval tapestry. The Kydds became quite famous in England, played London and the European capitals, kept honing their chops.

Harold Loomis wasn't happy. He wanted America. He'd closed the record store by now, goodnight dear old Papa, and become the full-time manager of the Kydds. He'd cultivated relationships with everyone from club promoters to disc jockeys, sound engineers to studio heads. That was how Harold liked to think of himself: as a cultivator. Hadn't he taken these four unpolished boys, young louts really, and nurtured them into a talented band with a number-one hit single? Now the label wanted an album. Harold wanted the label to send the Kydds on a tour of America.

And, no mistake, America was waiting. Its

bands were too bland, too bloated, or too black; as always, it wanted something it had never seen before. Its appetite for the Kydds turned out to be voracious.

You've probably seen the newsreels: the teenage girls clawing their way through police barricades, the Kydds coming down the flimsy metal staircase of an airplane, trying not to let the fear of crowd madness show through their good-natured smiles. The Union Jacks everywhere, and the giant cardboard heads of Peyton, Seth, Mark, or Dennis, each little girl's personal favorite. Peyton laughed at it, was flattered. Seth raged, said he didn't want a bunch of mindless cannibal-bitch Lolitas for fans. Harold said the little girls were all right to start with. They had money and influence. The serious listeners would catch on soon enough.

Seth told Harold he was insane to believe prepubescent girls had influence. A week later, though, when the banner of *The New York Times* read "KYDDS CONQUER USA," even Seth had to admit that Harold might know something he himself didn't.

"The men don't know, but the little girls understand," said Harold, smirking at Seth.

The concert changed the way they thought about everything. None of them, including Harold, had ever seen a crowd that size; they associated such crowds with coronations and other royal events. There was an instant of silence as they took the stage; then the screaming started again. They glanced at each other almost shyly, paralyzed until Dennis twirled a drumstick and touched it to a cymbal. When they launched into "Dig Your Man," they could hardly hear themselves. It wasn't the best show they had ever played, not by a long shot, but the sensation of the throng was unlike anything they'd ever imagined: deeper than sex, more primal than rock, seeming to happen in slow motion. They would play together onstage many more times, but never with the same unselfconscious sense of fun they'd had before. This show had put too much awe into them.

They saw very little of New York—the insides of luxurious hotel rooms, the bowels of a stadium. For "relaxation"—which, like everything else they did, was filmed—they were taken to Central Park one day. Seth stood on top of a great boulder and marveled at the view, unlike anything he'd ever seen before, wilderness surrounded by the peaks and spires of the city.

"Do you think you could ever live in America?" asked a reporter. As Harold hovered anxiously just out of frame, the others shook their heads: "No, no, don't think so. England's home." Seth, for once, kept quiet.

vi

The Kydds had just finished recording their second album—the first had been a series of their old cover songs arranged around "Cry My Tears Away" and "Dig your Man"—and Seth had broken up with a girlfriend from his Silver Dreams days, a girlfriend who wanted a great deal more than he could give to any one woman just now. So Seth thought little of it when Harold asked him to come on holiday to Amsterdam. He thought he deserved a holiday, and Harold would pay for everything, just like a proper manager. Seth had never been to Amsterdam, but Harold knew it well.

"You can get marijuana everywhere. They're even talking about legalizing it," Peyton said when Seth told him of the trip. They'd been turned on to pot ages ago, even before they'd moved to London; now they were famous, somebody was always hovering on the sidelines ready to show them a new kick. "Be careful of Harold, though."

"Whatever do you mean?"

"What do you think? He's queer, you know."

"So?"

"Well, nothing, but why's he taking you on holiday and not all four of us? You're his favorite, that's why. You're the butch one."

"He thinks of me as the group's leader."

"He wants you to lead *him,* most likely."

"Perhaps I will then," said Seth, just to see the look on Peyton's face.

Their hotel rooms looked out over a canal in the Red Light District. At night, the arches of the canal bridges were lit with red bulbs like half-open lipsticked mouths. They walked through the narrow streets looking slantwise at the girls behind the windows. "If you want to, you know, if you're thinking of having one, I'll just nip off for a bit," said Harold. There was a girl that had caught Seth's eye, Asian and bird-boned, but Harold sounded so miserable at the prospect that Seth just laughed it off. Instead they drank beer in a cafe stained with four hundred years' worth of nicotine, giving it a many-layered brown warmth such as Seth imagined the inside of a cocoon might have.

It was after two when they got back to the

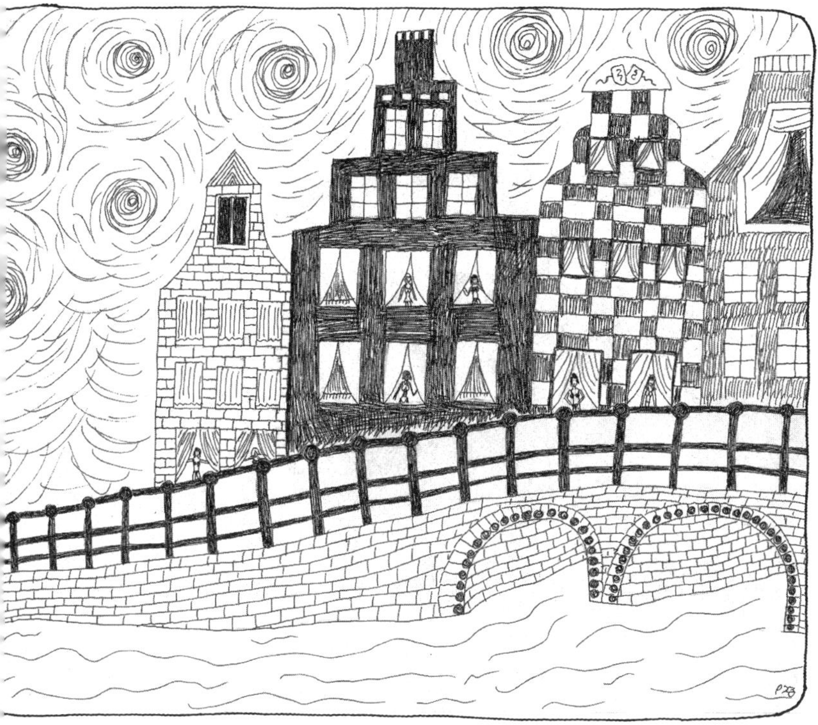

hotel. Seth climbed the winding staircase first, aware of Harold's eyes on him from below. At the landing, they turned to go to their separate rooms.

"Seth?"

"Yeah?"

A somehow strangled pause.

"Yeah, Harold?"

"Nothing."

Seth couldn't leave him like this. "Come in for a smoke. I've got some great weed."

"I've never had it..."

"Come on."

The smoke eased things, made Seth feel less like a high-priced rent boy and seemed to turn Harold into a less self-conscious version of himself. For half an hour or so, as they talked and laughed, sex was not even in the room. Then it was there again, in the set of Harold's shoulders and the way he could not stop looking at Seth.

"I'd better go," Harold said.

"What, back to your room? Why?"

"Because I want—something—"

"Didn't it ever occur to you that I might want something too?"

The expression on Harold's face would have been comical were his relief not so real. Seth sat on the edge of the bed. He couldn't pretend that, given his choice of men, he would have picked Harold Loomis. But Harold was smart and kind, even rather handsome in the right light, and Seth had always enjoyed bullying him. If Harold cooperated, which Seth felt sure he would, this could be quite fun.

Curiosity, after all, was what had always moved him forward in the world. And it hadn't done him a wrong turn yet.

Peyton didn't exactly disapprove of the relationship between Seth and Harold, but he worried about it. He knew he shouldn't worry, because there was nothing he could do about it, but that was exactly what he didn't like: a situation to do with the band that he couldn't control.

Mark and Dennis didn't care; Peyton had the idea that before meeting Harold they'd barely known what a homosexual was. Who Seth slept with was clearly none of their concern. Peyton was pretty sure no one knew about the affair but the other Kydds, Harold, and himself. Still he could not stop worrying.

When he asked Seth about it, Seth said it was a lot of fun but emotionally it meant nothing to either of them. Peyton knew that wasn't true for Harold, and he believed Seth knew it too. "Harold loves you," he said. "He's probably loved you since the day he met us."

"Harold's a big boy. He can look out for himself."

"He can look out for *us*. Himself, I'm not so sure of."

Seth just shrugged.

Peyton backed away from the subject, sensing that it made Seth uncomfortable. Perhaps that was good; if Seth was uncomfortable with the affair, he might just let it fizzle out. But then what would Harold do? Peyton worried, and worried some more.

It never once occurred to him that he might be jealous.

London in the mid-sixties, Seth decided, made Leyborough look like a gravesite. The really big money hadn't come rolling in yet, the checks with mind-bending numbers of zeroes they would see later, but already they had more than they'd ever seen in their lives. There was enough so that Harold had been able to set them all up in large convenient houses. The others had all bought cars—Peyton had a little Italian roadster that could go 150 miles per hour. The few times Seth tried driving a car, it terrified him greatly and his passengers more so. He rented a limo when it seemed necessary and took taxis the rest of the time.

He loved the bright swirl of Piccadilly Circus with its statue of Eros, the attention he got on Carnaby Street, the hidden perversions of Soho. He would come home with carloads of books, records, clothing, people. Impromptu parties sometimes went on for days. Seth would often disappear upstairs with a girl or boy—one about as often as the other now—returning hours later, ready for more. He felt young and strong and insatiable.

He had ten new guitars, all of them better than the shopworn janglebox he'd gotten for Christmas years ago back in Leyborough. But he kept the old guitar, the one he'd learned to play on, and wasn't surprised that Peyton had kept his old one too. For a certain kind of boy, his first guitar will always be more memorable than his first girl.

He'd slept with Harold a few more times, but his heart wasn't in it. He cared for Harold, and the sex was better than Seth had known it could ever be—Harold knew just where to touch, stroke, suck. It made sense, Seth supposed; a man would know how to handle another man's body. But something wasn't right. He didn't love Harold, but Harold loved him. In fact, Harold loved him almost like a mother. He'd thought he wanted that, but it was simply too weird to continue.

So he played hard in the great playground of London, and thought nothing of the pain in Harold's eyes, the new pain that came with Seth's brush-off and never went away. He stayed high on pot all day, realizing that it brought his anger down to a level where he could manage it, where he didn't want to kill somebody every single day of his life. He discovered lysergic acid, and it was good, very good. It showed him that he deserved this crazy, out-of-control fame as much as anyone on earth, that fame and money were ephemeral things one need not feel embarrassed to have, that he was just another plastic Jesus in a plastic world: a phrase that grew into a song he believed was one of his best. He turned the rest of the band on to acid, and the melting colors swirled through their next two albums, turning pop into a different creature, birthing a completely new sound into a world that also seemed increasingly new.

Mark bought an old instrument from the nineteen-twenties, something called a theremin. It was a black box with two antennae sticking out, and you played the thing without touching it—you just moved your hands around the instrument, creating shimmery phantom waves of sound. Seth was delighted to learn that its inventor, Leon Theremin, had at first been persecuted by his native Soviet Union but would later design secret electronics for their government. It was just the sort of contradiction he loved.

He went to a party with Peyton one night, a huge flat in Kings Road, lots of Americans and cocaine. They snorted lines off the cover of their third album and fell about laughing like everyone else. Somebody took a picture that night that they ended up using, along with many others, on the inner sleeve of the next album: arms around each other's shoulders, cheeks pressed together, identical fucked-up grins on their faces.

Later, Seth would remember this time in London with nostalgia: nothing to compete with the time when his mother was alive, but nostalgia nonetheless. He would remember it more precisely as the last time that was really his own, the time before things went insane.

Because soon, oh, soon it was all too much. He remembered his grandmother calling something "much of a muchness," and though she'd probably meant something quite different, that was exactly what it felt like.

The world wasn't just America and London and Amsterdam now; it was Australia, Germany, the Phillipines, Japan, and all were a mass of writhing, screaming little girls. Japan was where it all went wrong for Seth somehow. This might have had something to do with the ten hits of blotter acid he'd smuggled through customs in his rock star bag. The rock star bag seemed to be taken for granted by customs inspectors the world over. It was simply a small bag the rock star carried on his person, and no one ever looked inside it. The very first time they'd gone overseas, Harold had told them, "Do *not* bring anything illegal, but if you must bring something *questionable,* be sure to pack it in your in-flight bag."

From then on, their in-flight bags were known to the Kydds as rock star bags, and all manner of illicit substances traveled back and forth in them. "What have you got in your rock star bag today then, Peyt?" "Oh, nothing much, Dennis, nothing that would get you arrested in Singapore." Nonetheless, some paranoia impelled Seth to get rid of the ten hits of acid before leaving Japan, and the only acceptable method of doing this was to eat them all at once.

Locked in a small room with black lacquer fixtures and rice paper walls, he began to freak. He started dialing room numbers. Harold was out. So was Peyton. No one else seemed to be in the hotel. His throat tightened painfully; the air swirled with colorful motes. From somewhere far below, he could hear screaming. He crawled into bed and piled all the pillows over his ears, and he could still hear the screaming, shrill and incessant. A vivid hallucination took shape in his mind, a scene from Goya going on seventeen floors down. Someone had built an enormous funeral pyre and the little girls were throwing themselves onto it, twisting in the flames like medieval martyrs, burning and screaming. That was it, that was the symbol. His entire career had been built on the pain of thwarted little girls, and everywhere he went, more girls were begging for it, elbowing each other aside to be the first to die screaming in agony as a demonstration of love for him. In his head, a girl swallowed a box of tacks; her sister drank a gallon of lye. An Australian girl shot herself in the guts. A creative lassie in Scotland tied her four limbs to four strong horses...

And they never stopped screaming.

The door slammed open. The sound brought Seth back to the hotel room. Peyton stood in the doorway, a Japanese schoolgirl dangling from each arm. "Around the world to the sound of screams, eh, Sethy? These two were asking for you—"

The little girls caught sight of Seth, naked on the bed wrapped in a sheet, brains fizzing out his ears, and they both started to scream. And Seth sat up and screamed back at them, screamed and SCREAMED into their avid, empty faces until his throat was raw—

No. There were no Japanese schoolgirls in the room, no girls at all. Peyton was on the bed with him, gathering him up like an armload of laundry. "You didn't take all that blotter, did you? Oh Christ, of course you did. Right, let's just be quiet."

He lay with his head in Peyton's lap while Peyton sang him a disjointed sort of lullaby, though they both knew he would not sleep, and gradually the screaming faded away.

"Oh Peyt," he said. "Oh Peyt. I don't know if I can take it."

Peyton nodded. "It's too much, isn't it? I think this should be our last tour."

"You mean... ?" Seth could not articulate what he thought Peyton might mean.

"I don't mean break up the band, if that's what you thought. But why keep going on these tours?

Harold wants us to, but we don't need the money, and we can't hear ourselves onstage anyway. I thought we could sort of retire from touring, stay together in the studio, make records. We don't need to do this any more."

As the truth of what Peyton was saying struck him, Seth felt both incredibly relieved and utterly spent. He buried his face in the pillows. When he could speak again, he said, "That's just what I want to do. Thanks, Peyt."

"Now *there's* something I don't hear often enough from you."

"Harold won't like it, though."

"Harold's not the boss any more."

Harold's not lots of things any more, Seth thought. But he could not follow the thought to its logical conclusion. Peyton's presence beside him was one friendly and comforting thing in a world that had nearly come apart at the seams tonight. He groped for Peyton's hand, enfolded Peyton's callused fingers in his own, and actually managed to drift into some sort of sleep. His dreams were unnaturally colorful and too disturbing to remember, but when he woke, his friend was still beside him, their hands still intertwined.

vii

Peyton got the news from Dennis late one night. Harold had picked up the wrong bit of rough trade, apparently, at the beginning of a weekend when no one expected to hear from him for at least forty-eight hours. He'd been found in his flat by his cleaning woman, beaten, broken, and beginning to rot. The flat had been stripped of valuables; whatever hadn't been stolen was smashed. Peyton's first thought was of Seth. "Has anyone told him yet?" he asked.

"I don't know. I haven't talked to him. You think he's tripping?"

"He's always tripping," Peyton said glumly, and hung up the phone. He put his jacket back on and drove to Seth's house. On the way he thought only vaguely of Harold. He'd somehow assumed something like this would happen to Harold one day. He thought of how Harold had wanted them, wanted especially Seth so much, had had Seth but not in any way that mattered. So he'd filled that void with unpredictable trash that had eventually, inevitably killed him.

He let himself into Seth's house with the key he had. They'd always had keys to each other's places, ever since their school days, and never questioned the fact. This new place in Knightsbridge was huge, the floor plan convoluted, and even though he had been there several times he had to wander a bit before he found the main bedroom. If Seth knew that Harold had died, then Seth would be in bed. Seth's response to anything that exercised his emotions had always been to go to bed.

He was there, of course, the long lean shape of him twisted beneath sweaty covers. He was awake, blinking slowly. Peyton sat on the edge of the bed. "Who called you?"

"Mark."

That wasn't so bad; Mark was always rather diffident with Seth, and would have broken it to him gently. But there was no good way for Seth to have gotten this news. He'd be feeling so many things about it, and none of them in harmony with each other: blaming himself, not without some cause, though of course you couldn't really think of it that way, and maybe even relieved because the whole messy business of fucking Harold would be done with, and then blaming himself for this relief... No, there was really no good side to it at all.

Seth knew Peyton was sitting there analyzing Seth's emotional state, gauging his reaction to the news, maybe even wondering how soon they'd be able to get back into the studio, and this calculation made him sick. Yet Peyton was the person he needed right now, more than anyone else in the world. He hadn't thought losing Harold could hurt so much, thought he'd lost the capacity for this kind of pain after his mother's death. His mind was feverish with *What if he...* and *If I only*. He knew he needed Peyton even though it infuriated him to have this need, and he reached for Peyton's hand, aware that his own hand was clammy with sweat and tears but not caring.

When Peyton felt Seth's hand clutching his own, something in him melted. He climbed all the way onto the bed and pulled Seth into his arms, cradled him through the bedclothes as best he could. Seth sagged against him and sobbed, a dry, wrenching sound, that of a man unused to crying. "Oh Christ," he said at last. "Oh, Peyt. I did this to him. I did."

"You didn't. Some random piece of shit did."

"But I knew... I *knew*..." Seth couldn't go on for a minute. Then he said, "I knew he used to pick up rough trade. I knew it was dangerous. But I let him go back to it."

"What could you do, Seth? You couldn't stay with him out of pity. You didn't love him."

"I *did* love him. Just not the way he wished I did."

"I know," said Peyton. "I know."

They were silent for a while. Seth's next whisper was so soft that Peyton missed its meaning. "What?"

"I love *you* that way," Seth said.

Peyton was glad of the room's darkness then; it hid the blood that rose to his cheeks. "You don't," he said.

"I *do*. You came here... only you came here... and I thought... oh, *Christ*..." Seth punched a pillow in frustration as he began to sob again.

"Shhh. Shhh, Seth. You thought what?"

"I thought: *I can get through this*. I can get through it with Harold. But if it was *you*..."

"Well, it wouldn't be me, would it?" Peyton said reasonably. "I don't do the things Harold did."

"Not any of them?"

"What d'you—"

Seth stopped Peyton's mouth with a kiss.

Peyton's heart began to hammer in his chest. He pulled back, looked closely at Seth, whose face was full of naked hope. Peyton ran though his immediate reactions and found no revulsion, some curiosity, but most of all a sense that he could do this if it needed to be done. That was what he'd always done for Seth, really—whatever needed to be done for him. An irresistible hook for a song that was a little too raw. A lyric for a wordless riff. A fiver, a word of diplomacy with the suits at the record company, a lift home back in Leyborough when Seth was too drunk to stand. Whatever Seth needed, that was what Peyton did, and if the reason was because Seth was the only person with whom he could write great music—well, that was a kind of love as true as any.

He put his other hand to Seth's face, brushed hair out of Seth's swollen eyes. He stretched out on the bed and gathered Seth closer to him. Not until they kissed a second time, with open mouths like lovers, did Peyton understand that this act was irrevocable.

This would change everything between them, and Seth was afraid. But he'd been afraid for a long time and he was sick of it, sick of this new peaceful acid-tamed version of himself, and he suddenly wanted this as much as he had ever wanted anything. It was funny; he'd never once thought of Peyton that way, not even after he realized he liked boys as well as girls. Of course he knew Peyton was a good-looking bastard, anybody could see that. But he was *Peyton*, little

Peyton Masters who'd astonished him in Leyborough by being able to play the guitar as well as Seth despite looking like a posh choirboy, Peyton with whom he'd shared a thousand squalid hotel rooms, train cars, toilets down the corridor. Just Peyton.

He touched his friend warily, certain that at any moment he would be stopped. Peyton was as straight as a ruler; he'd certainly made that clear enough to Harold early on. But Peyton did not stop him.

He wondered if Harold's ghost might be somewhere nearby, hovering in a corner of the room perhaps, pleased at least that his death had brought his boys to this room, this moment.

It was all so slow, so easy. *Languid;* the word came lazily into Peyton's mind as they held each other, barely moving. He'd thought everything that happened between two men would be as hard and urgent as the cocks that drove them, but this was something else, something like moving into another, previously unknown level of friendship. He felt light-headed, not quite serious—this was, after all, *Seth*—but also very aroused, much more so than he had expected. He'd expected it to be a comfort for Seth, maybe a blowjob for himself—a man's mouth couldn't feel much different from a woman's. Nothing more.

Instead it was like a brand-new passion finally given voice, a thing with no urgency and no awkwardness, just a need they both knew how to fill. Sometimes they laughed at the incredibility of it. Sometimes they cried. Toward dawn they fell into a long healing sleep, and woke hours later still intertwined, feeling reborn.

Neither of them had previously been quick to commit to anything that might be called love, despite the number of women who'd been anxious to bag them—increasingly so as the fame and the money got bigger. Yet somehow, from that night on, Peyton and Seth knew they were together. It wasn't so different from before, really; for a long time theirs had been a marriage of sorts.

At first, it was astonishing how little their lives changed. Already there was no need to manage money; it turned out that Harold had taken a bit more than his share of their early contracts, but he had willed that share, along with all his other worldly goods, to Seth. So they kept both houses, but usually stayed at Seth's because it was closer to the center of London. The house became a cocoon for them, a fantasy castle from which they emerged occasionally to buy food or fill social obligations. Those first few months were like nothing so much as a reprise of when they'd first met, their new intoxication with each other similar to that time, though it came from a different source.

Mark and Dennis knew. There was no way anyone who had much contact with Peyton and Seth could fail to know. They didn't seem to mind, and what if they had? The fans, the press, and most of all the four musicians knew that Peyton and Seth were the heart and brain of the Kydds: Mark and Dennis weren't about to walk out on a gold mine just because their bandmates were sucking each other's cocks.

But the news of their relationship hadn't hit the media yet. It was the first time in his career that Peyton was uncertain of his ability to charm his way through a potential mess. It was 1967, homosexuality had just been decriminalized in Britain, and gay relationships were better accepted than they had ever been before, but that still wasn't saying much. Certainly Harold Loomis had received little sympathy from any quarter. There had been no real police effort to catch the murderer, despite a £50,000 reward offered by the band. The public consensus seemed to be that Harold was a vile predator who had somehow taken advantage of the loveable Kydds, and in being beaten to death by a fellow pervert, he'd only gotten what he deserved.

If the press got hold of this other thing, Peyton wasn't sure he and Seth would still have careers. But Seth would never keep quiet; Seth was all

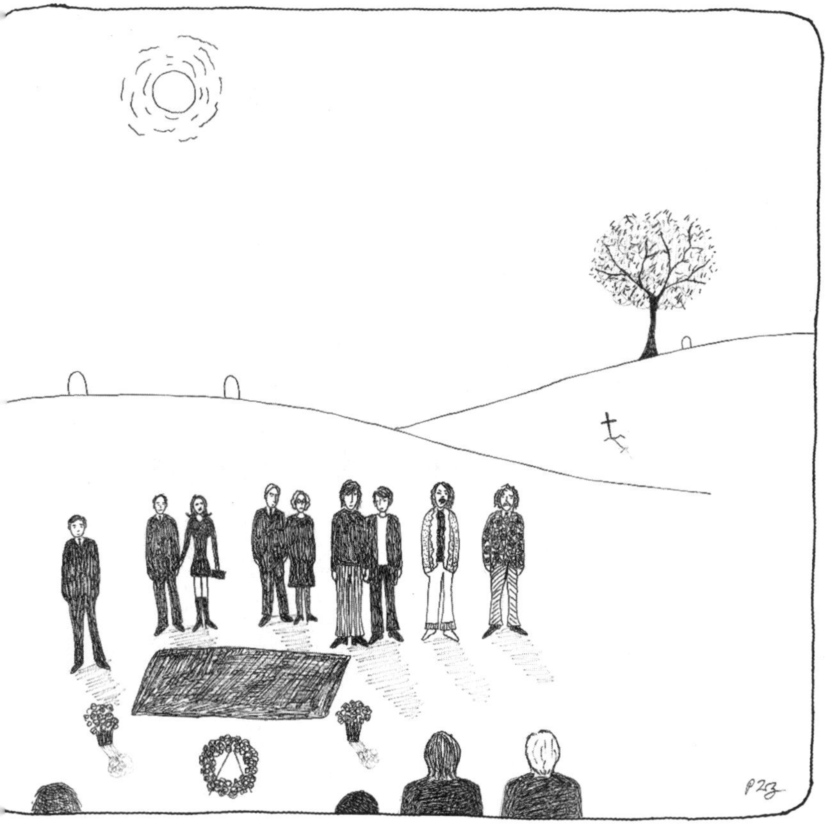

about not keeping quiet. In fact, Seth wanted to call a press conference.

"This is who we are, Peyt. This is us. Does it feel like something that ought to be hidden?"

"No, but—"

"Fuck it then. If people hate queers so much, let them hate us. We've made our money. Let the fame go."

That wasn't so easy for Peyton to think about. He liked the fame much more than Seth ever had, and Seth knew it. "I don't want to sit on my ass and count the money we've made. I want to keep making music."

"We *will* make music—with or without Dennis and Mark. People can decide for themselves whether it's as good as before."

They'll say it isn't, Peyton thought. *Even if it's the best music we've ever made, you know they'll say it isn't.* He wondered if he was right or just afraid.

Harold's funeral was private, but of course the press got in. When you were big enough, the press always got in. Seth knew that was one thing he wouldn't miss about fame if it left him.

At the graveside, he reached over and took Peyton's hand. Flashbulbs went off in the distance. Seth wondered how much even the London paparazzi could make of two friends holding hands at a third friend's funeral.

Well, he promised himself, *if they try to make anything of it, I'll give them more than they bargained for.*

But nothing came of those photos. So Peyton worried, and Seth watched television. In this paleolithic era of technology, he had managed to purchase a device that would change the channels at the press of a button, so that he could sit cross-legged and naked in bed flipping through them for hours. From the cathode torrent he gleaned song lyrics and bits of obscure knowledge.

Peyton always made sure there were plenty of good drugs around: acid, weed of stratospheric quality, occasional downers. Sometimes Seth thought Peyton was trying to keep him quiet by keeping him stoned. Sometimes he thought it was working. The drugs made him feel cozy and contented. The pain of Harold's death began to fade, and Seth wondered why he had ever wanted to throw away such a perfect life for the sake of a principle. He'd never considered his romantic relationships public business before; why should that change now? He was happy with Peyton. The loving was great, the music was great, and every-

LUNCH
BANNED!
URS
THE CARLETON
PARIS
Rx
Seth Grealy
Tuinal
Take as need
The Groove
LONDON
THE NAKED
CIVIL SERVA
QUENTIN CRISP

one was nice to them everywhere they went. If he told, how much of that would change?

So when somebody offered him a line of heroin at a party, Seth snorted it with no hesitation. He liked it a lot, and soon managed to get some more. As long as he didn't inject it, he couldn't get a habit; he kept telling himself that like a mantra. Heroin was the final step in the warm-safe-Mummy equation he'd been trying to solve for years. Seth felt as if he would never need to worry about anything again.

Peyton didn't approve of heroin, which didn't stop him from trying it once. They lay curled together on their bed, swathed in cashmere blankets, floating on the warm narcotic sea. "It *is* awfully nice," Peyton admitted. "Too nice. No wonder you never get anything done anymore."

"I've written two songs this month."

"You used to write ten a month."

"Fuck you, Peyt. Can't you just enjoy a thing?"

"I can," Peyton said. "For now, I can." He propped himself on one elbow and began to kiss Seth deeply. For a few hours the problems went away.

In this manner, two years passed. The Kydds released two new albums, each marking a major growth not just in their music but in the concept of rock music itself. Or so the critics said. The Kydds themselves never quite stopped feeling like four ne'er-do-wells from Leyborough, and in their weaker moments they supposed the world would see through them eventually, but in the meantime they intended to have fun. Mark and Dennis had their money, their girls. Seth had his happy home and his little low-grade habit. And Peyton, as he'd wished for long ago, had everything.

viii

By 1969, Peyton didn't worry as much as he used to, but Seth still watched a great deal of TV. He watched commercials, cartoon shows, body counts from the war in Vietnam all with equal absorption. That summer he saw something that would change both their lives.

Seth had become something of a recluse in these past two years. If the Kydds weren't in the studio, Seth was usually in bed. He had a never-ending stack of books, a bunch of daily newspapers from all over the world, his cigar box full of drugs, his mirror and razor blades and rolling papers. And, of course, the TV. If Peyton was in the house, Seth was always yelling at him to come here *right now,* Peyt, you've gotta see this. But it was usually something interesting. This time it was more interesting than usual.

The BBC was showing a news clip of a riot in

New York. At first Peyton thought it was a race riot. Then he saw that the rioters were of all different races, and that many of the men were in drag. They were jeering at policemen, throwing rocks and bottles. As Seth and Peyton watched, a policeman jumped back into his patrol car and peered out at the crowd, looking almost comically terrified.

Seth filled in the blanks. A gay bar in Greenwich Village, the Stonewall Inn, had been raided by the police. In America, gay bars weren't illegal in theory, but in practice they could be raided at any time and the patrons arrested on morals charges. Usually those who weren't arrested slunk away, hoping to escape the notice of the police. This time, apparently, they hadn't.

For the first time in he wasn't sure how long, Peyton thought of Harold. How many places had *he* been forced to slink away from in his short life?

Some of the young men in front of the Stonewall Inn were shirtless. They draped themselves over one another and kissed for the cameras. They were reckless and gorgeous. They looked the way Peyton had felt when the Kydds first started up, when he hadn't cared about anything but playing loud American rock and roll.

"We have to go there!" Seth said.

With an effort, Peyton dragged his eyes away from the screen and looked at his partner. Seth was thinner than he'd been in years. His eyes

A Spaniard in the Wor
THE OCTOBER COUNTRY
The Story of the Eye · BATAILLE
Django Reinhardt - A Life
INN
GRETSCH
Miss Thing

glittered hectically. God only knew how many things he was high on right now. But he was also excited, excited about doing something that involved leaving the house, excited in a way Peyton hadn't seen him get lately.

He knew that he hadn't discouraged Seth's heroin habit as he should have. Seth mightn't be writing as much as he used to, but the songs he did write were among the best he'd ever done. With Seth on smack, Peyton could have his partner, his lover, his band, and his peace all rolled into one. Seth hadn't felt like giving interviews, let alone holding press conferences, for quite some time now. Peyton handled most of the publicity. If pressed about his personal life, he said he was seeing an actress.

He looked back at the TV and felt a deep stab of shame.

"We have to go," Seth said again.

Peyton sat on the edge of the bed, slid his arm around Seth's waist, leaned his head against Seth's. "Yeah," he said finally, "I suppose we do."

They were only there a little while before the glut of fans and media got so thick that they had to leave for their own safety. But in this case, a little while was enough.

They'd left London that very night, arrived in New York the next morning, slept all afternoon at the St. Regis, then gone down to the Village. The rioting was over, the bar closed for the moment, but people were still congregating in front of the Stonewall Inn. The summer evening was clear and blue, the smell of sweat intoxicating. This had become a pilgrimage spot, no less to Seth and Peyton than any of the others.

They stood on the sidewalk talking to people, their arms slung casually round each other like so many other pairs of young men on this hot summer evening. "Aren't you Seth Grealy and Peyton Masters?" someone finally asked, half-embarrassed—New Yorkers were supposed to be so cool about celebrities—and they said yes.

Someone else asked the question that would become a cliché: "Are you two, uh, *together?*"

Everyone laughed—perhaps it was already a cliché—and they could have dodged the question that time. But they just said yes again, and the love that engulfed them from this crowd seemed much more genuine than anything they'd ever felt on a stage.

What would become, arguably, their most famous interview was captured on tape by a reporter who'd been drinking down the street at the Lion's Head. Someone in the crowd filmed them with a small movie camera as they spoke. The reporter and the cameraman would later pair up, sell their footage for a small fortune, and spend the next decade traveling through Asia.

REPORTER: So what brings the Kydds to the Village?

SETH: It's just us two. We came because of Stonewall. We saw it on TV and thought, you know, we have to come. Because of our relationship.

REPORTER: What relationship?

SETH (unable to resist batting his eyes a bit): He's my boyfriend.

REPORTER: Peyton?

PEYTON: "Boyfriend" isn't the word I would choose, but yes, we've been together for two years, and it's only our own prejudices that have caused us to lie about it. What's happened here gave us courage we should have had sooner.

(He is nearly drowned out by raucous cheering from the crowd.)

REPORTER: What will your fans think? Aren't you afraid of the effect this will have on your career?

SETH: Personally I don't give a fuck. Anyway we've got less to lose than most of the people who rioted here.

PEYTON: You can't live your whole life being afraid of the effect things will have...

SETH: You bleedin' well can! Most people do! Our manager did, you know, and they killed him for it. But not us. Not any more. Peyton's always been my musical partner. Now he's my life partner. Your country's at war—call this our contribution to peace.

(More noise from the crowd.)

REPORTER: Are the Kydds still a band?

PEYTON: We'll find out when we get home, won't we?

But they did not go home yet. Their New York visit stretched out to days, then weeks. Occasionally someone would say something nasty to them on the streets, but this happened less often than they had expected. More frequently they got grins, thumbs-up, power salutes. They could not believe that their mere presence had changed the tenor of feelings about Stonewall, but given the public reaction, they could not discount that possibility either.

Their first interview as a couple had been impromptu. After that, they chose their outlets carefully. They were not afraid to argue their case, but they knew from experience how words and even film clips could be twisted to fit an agenda.

Seth was still taking a lot of drugs, but he was also getting out, exploring the city, talking to people. Maybe it was just freedom from the burden of a secret, but the New York Seth seemed more fully alive than the man Peyton had known in London. He wondered if politics might be a galvanizing force for Seth, a less destructive catalyst than heroin.

At the end of their first month in New York they accepted an invitation to appear on the cover of *Newsweek*. The accompanying story was favorable, if a bit mystified in tone: the female reporter who interviewed them could not imagine how two rich and famous musicians who had women practically crawling through their windows could choose to be with each other instead. Seth's explanation that it was not so much choice as destiny seemed to have gone right over her head. But, the article went on, if two such beloved public figures had decided to go public with their homosexuality in the wake of the Stonewall riots, then perhaps it was time to consider homosexuality in a different light.

"That's the sentence that makes the rest of the crap worthwhile," Seth told Peyton, pointing to the page in the magazine. "That's the kind of thing that can change people's thinking. If it's going to be all about celebrity worship, we have to take advantage of that."

Peyton noticed that Seth was cutting back on the drugs, sometimes going a day or more without doing a line of heroin and almost giving up the LSD altogether. The spate of nasty reader mail *Newsweek* published in its next issue didn't faze him. Nor did reports from the Bible Belt that Kydds records and paraphernalia were being banned on radio, returned by stores, and thrown onto enormous bonfires organized by fundamentalist church groups. It was a heady time when nothing seemed to matter much, until the telegram arrived from London.

WHY NOT CONSULT US BEFORE GOING PUBLIC? WE SUPPORTED YOU IN THIS, NOW YOU ABANDON US. SUPPOSED TO BE IN STUDIO BUT HALF OUR BAND IS MISSING. MAYBE KYDDS ARE NO LONGER A VIABLE REALITY. MARK AND DENNIS.

Peyton's first reaction was guilt. For the first time in the history of the Kydds, he had failed to acknowledge the democracy of the band, creating a situation that couldn't be finessed or smoothed over. He knew they should have warned Mark and Dennis that they were going public, but it had been such a spur-of-the-moment, gut-reaction thing that he honestly hadn't thought of it. He knew that he and Seth should be back in

London by now, back in the studio recording the next album, but they had become so happy in New York that they hadn't wanted to deal with the idea of going home.

The next week, they flew back to London to see whether the mess could be dealt with. But Seth refused to admit any wrong, and soon he wasn't speaking to Mark and Dennis at all. Instead he returned to bed, redoubled his drug use, and swore that he would never again be known as a Kydd.

Peyton was left to meet with Mark, Dennis, and various representatives of the record company. They had never hired a new manager after Harold died, and even if they had, Peyton doubted if any manager could have helped much. He pulled out diplomatic stops he'd never known he had, but nothing seemed to matter. Eventually he came to believe that Mark and Dennis' resentment was a visceral matter that had little to do with business or even music.

"It's all very well for you two," Mark summed up during one bitter argument. "When fans think of the Kydds, they think of you. You'll be able to go off and do whatever you like. We'll just be a washed-up rhythm section who are probably a couple of queers."

"Why would you care so much if people thought that?" Peyton asked, realizing only after he spoke that Seth had posed much the same question to him two years ago. But Mark could not explain, and Dennis didn't care to try either. Probably they didn't even know.

Slowly, amidst countless disputes that pretended to be about money but were really about something much sadder, the band was dissolved. It remained Peyton's only real regret from that time: if the Kydds could not have gone on forever, he wished they might have been allowed to die a decent death instead of an ugly and protracted lynching.

As soon as it was done, he and Seth returned to New York. They both knew they would never live in England again.

They stayed in Greenwich Village for a year, until wanderlust seized them again. Their tours of Europe with the Kydds had been much like their first trip to New York: except for Seth's trip to Amsterdam with Harold, they hadn't seen much save the insides of hotels and stadia. Now they would see it all. As well, there was a rumor Seth had heard and wanted to investigate: in Holland, though the ceremony was not legally binding elsewhere, there was a renegade excommunicated priest who would marry two people of the same sex. It turned out to be true, and handily enough, the ex-priest also ran one of Amsterdam's newly legal cannabis coffeeshops.

"That was the kiss heard round the world,"

said Peyton afterward. The ceremony in the coffeeshop was private, with a small enclave of friends that conspicuously did not include Mark and Dennis, but reporters gathered outside to snap pictures as they emerged. The photo most printed, of course, was of Seth and Peyton kissing on the stone steps of the three-hundred-year-old building; the most prevalent headline, "THEY DO!"

Not content to honeymoon, they began recording a new album in a Paris studio. They would never really have a proper band again—they would always be just Grealy and Masters, with whatever session players they needed for the few instruments they couldn't play between them. It had been too painful losing the Kydds. They didn't ever want to break up another band.

For five years they shuttled back and forth between Europe and New York, making music and doing benefit concerts, stopping in England occasionally but never for long. At last, though, the craziness of their time with the Kydds seemed to catch up with them and they needed calm. It wouldn't have been the obvious choice for most people, but for them, calmness and peace of mind were in New York City. They applied for permanent U.S. residence, bought a huge apartment in a Gothic horror of a building on the Upper West Side, and moved in for good.

ix

The story had come full circle. Peyton sat curled in Dr. Jonathan Pumphrey's big leather chair, his knees drawn up to his chest. His eyelashes appeared wet, but he had not used any of the Kleenex.

"And how long ago was that—that you moved to New York?" Jonathan asked.

"Ten years. You know what we've been doing since then, I suppose. We kept recording for a while, but eventually we felt we'd done all we could in the public eye. We could hear our influence in new music, and that was enough. So we retired."

"But you never stopped playing music."

"Oh, God, no. That was as much a part of our lives as making love—well, for us, it was a kind of making love. Seth had gotten really good on the piano and I was doing some classical guitar stuff. We'd even talked about recording again. Just for fun—nothing that was going to change the world."

"You and Seth already changed it," Jonathan reminded.

"Yes, he disliked hearing it, but I think we did. Let me tell you something, though, Dr. Pumphrey: I'd trade it all to have him back again."

Jonathan could think of no suitable reply to this.

"I'll leave you soon. I just have one more question for you. I feel soft, asking such a thing, but I honestly don't know any more. Do you think he was ever really happy?"

"Yes. These past years with you, here in New York, I think he was."

"Then I want one thing from you."

"Of course; anything I can do—"

"This isn't a normal request, Doctor. I told you I didn't know why I'd come here. I was lying. I wanted to meet you, get an idea who you were, and see what you thought about Seth. Then, if it seemed all right, I planned to ask you for one thing. Well, I'm asking. I want you to get me close to Ray Brinker."

Jonathan opened his mouth, then shut it again. He had no idea what he'd been expecting, but it wasn't this.

"I'm Seth's official heir and the executor of his estate. As such, I'm entitled to mount a case against Brinker, aid the prosecution, even sue him for wrongful death if it comes to that. I've already discussed this with my lawyers. I can hire a psychiatrist to examine him for the purpose of determining his mental state. I want to hire you, and I want to go with you when you examine him."

"Peyton—I—no. This just can't work."

"Why not?"

"Well, if it's some kind of vendetta you have in mind, there's no way you could even get a weapon past security—"

Peyton spread his hands, widened his eyes. "No vendetta. I just want to talk to him. I want to know why."

"He told the media why. Wasn't that ugly enough? Do you want to hear him say it again?"

"Yes. I want to hear him say it to me."

"And the conflict of interest—me examining Brinker after being Seth's therapist for five years—"

"Could you at least get in?"

"I don't know. Maybe."

"If you can, will you take me?"

Jonathan looked at Peyton. Those big brown eyes widened further, protesting innocence, seeming to glitter with unshed tears. This man had loved Seth deeply and truly. Of that, Jonathan had no doubt.

"All right," he said finally. *"If* I can get in, I'll take you with me."

"You can get in. You can examine him tomorrow. It's already arranged. And of course we'll need to discuss your fee." Peyton named a sum that would pay the rent on Jonathan's midtown office for a year.

As Peyton let himself out, Jonathan sat with his head in his hands. He felt poleaxed. Every day he passed people living on the street in refrigerator boxes, for Christ's sake; he'd always thought of himself as well off. Now, for the first time, the curtain had been drawn aside and he had seen the smooth machinations of what real money could do.

It was another weird kind of dissonance for Jonathan, riding across the bridge to Riker's Island in Peyton's limousine. It wasn't a *stretch* limo or anything, but it was a hell of a lot nicer than any other car Jonathan had ever ridden in. Along for the ride was one of Peyton's lawyers, a pit bull of a man in a merino wool suit.

Jonathan had to keep his emotions on a tight rein while examining Ray Brinker. The doughy-faced killer neither protested his innocence nor admitted any remorse for his actions. Quite the contrary, he seemed to think he had done humanity a favor. "Nothing wrong with one less fag in the world" was a common refrain. Jonathan emerged from the interview convinced that the man was legally sane and prepared to testify so in court.

Only then was Peyton allowed into the room.

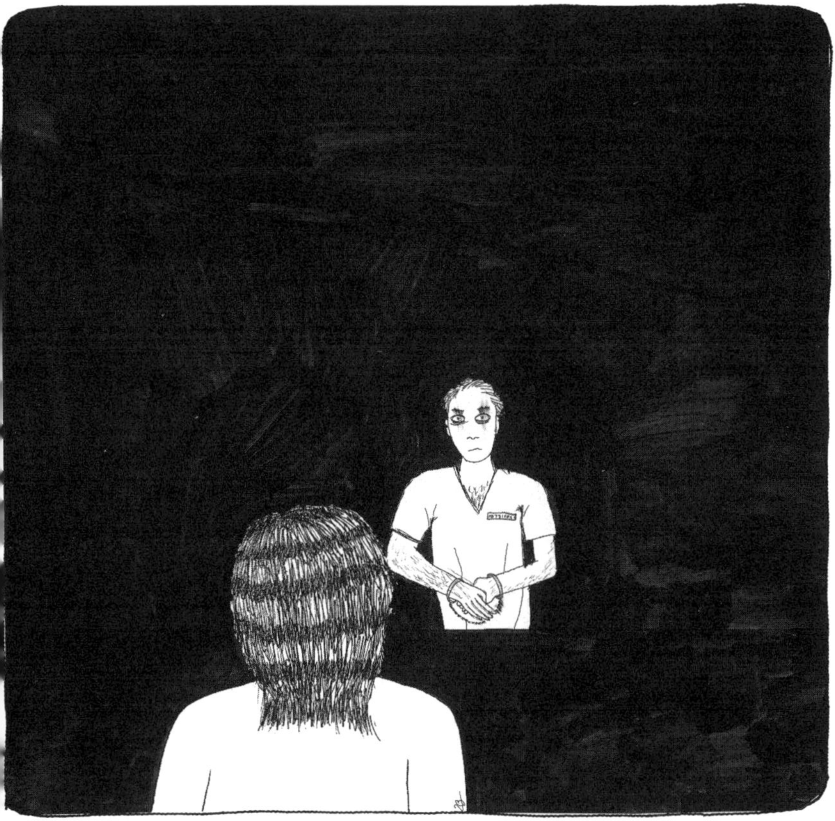

He did not invite Jonathan to stay, nor did he bring his lawyer in; but there were two armed prison guards present, so Peyton would not have been able to injure Brinker even if he had managed to smuggle a weapon past security. But Peyton did not seem inclined to violence. He simply stood before the killer and spoke quietly to him for several minutes as Jonathan and the lawyer watched through two layers of scratched and smeary Plexiglass. The contrast between the two men was striking: Brinker in cuffs and leg irons, prison-grimed, anger wrenching his pudgy body into a strange shape, his face not so much unattractive as *unfinished*-looking (Jonathan thought the man looked rather like a fetus); Peyton slim and clean and straight-spined, his beauty exaggerated in this place of ugliness, his face calm, almost serene.

He finished speaking to Brinker, made a little bow, and turned to leave the room. The guards parted for him, and one stopped him to ask for an autograph. The psychiatrist, the lawyer, and the rock star rode home in silence.

Jonathan was hardly surprised when he saw the headline the next morning: **GREALY'S ASSASSIN KILLS SELF IN PRISON**. Despite the usual precautions—and, given public sentiment about this case, Jonathan doubted whether there had been many of the usual precautions—Brinker had fashioned his pants into a kind of noose and hanged himself in his cell.

Jonathan would not have dreamed of telephoning Peyton. But when he received Peyton's call that night, it surprised him little more than the headline had done.

"Thank you for getting me in," said Peyton without preamble. "I'm not sure I could have gone on without that."

"I think you can do just about anything you decide to do," said Jonathan.

A short silence, not an angry one. "You may be right," Peyton said finally. "I'd love to think you are. In this case, anyway, I did what I had to do. Nothing more."

Jonathan's curiosity overcame his professional reserve. "What in the world did you say to him?"

"I simply told him that he'd given Seth the thing he wanted most: a martyr's death. He turned Seth into a kind of queer angel. Before, people looked at us and saw a happy couple—and that was good—but now they see a grieving lover and a martyred angel. It will give them courage. It will show them that love is worth dying for. Do you know what the last thing I said to him was, Dr. Pumphrey?"

"What?"

"I told him that this was the proof we needed. This was the proof that we really did change the world. And then I thanked him."

"You thanked him? You *thanked* him for killing Seth?"

"Oh, it was difficult to get those words out of

my mouth. You've no idea how difficult. But look what happened.

"It worked."

The receiver on Peyton's end was replaced with a soft click, and Jonathan was left holding the phone, holding the whole damn story, and wondering just what Seth Grealy had really died for.

YES, I WOULD
The author's afterword to *Plastic Jesus*

John Lennon was killed in New York when I was thirteen. I'd been aware of the Beatles before 1980, as if it were possible not to be. But the media coverage of John's death stoked my imagination, and obviously continues to do so today.

The first piece I published on this subject was the essay "Would You?" which you may have received as a free mini-chapbook if you bought the limited hardcover edition of this book. Though it has seen print before, I think it is a good companion to *Plastic Jesus,* and goes a long way toward explaining how this longer and more convoluted tale came to be.

If you didn't get the mini-chapbook, all you really need (besides love) is to know that I've been obsessed with the Beatles, and particularly John, for quite a long time. After his death, I bought a few records, then bought a few more, and eventually plastered my room with Beatles posters and became a teenage hippie Beatlemaniac—quite an anomaly in a rural North Carolina high school in the early eighties. John was the latest and best in a long line of attitude-driven badasses I admired. He inspired me to start an underground newspaper, reconsider my own political and social beliefs, experiment with drugs (something I'm quite happy with, thanks), and generally become an in-your-face rebel quite a few years earlier then I might have done otherwise.

Today I have John's cartoony little self-portrait tattooed on my left bicep. People have wondered aloud whether I will get sick of it, but in twenty years I've never gotten sick of the Beatles, and so far it's only been comforting to have him around, even if he is just a few lines of black ink under the skin of my arm. More to the point, I have always believed the world would be a better place today if John and Paul had been lovers. Yes, I *know* they weren't gay. That has nothing to do with it. This is a *fantasy*.

A couple of years ago, Bill Schafer of Subterranean Press asked to publish a chapbook of my work. I didn't have anything new of sufficient length, but I had long been interested in publishing my untitled 1987 novella that eventually grew into *Lost Souls*. I didn't think it was a great work of literature, but I believed fans of the novel would be interested to see the genesis of the story and how it had evolved. Bill said OK, and this became *The Seed of Lost Souls,* illustrated to perfection by Dame Darcy of *Meatcake* comics fame. I enjoyed the whole experience so much that when Bill asked me to do another book, this one a ten- to fifteen-thousand word piece of original fiction, I said yes.

At that time, I'd been working on my fifth novel for about a year and getting increasingly frustrated with it. There were some things I loved about it, but there were *a lot* of things I hated about it. When I threw out all the things I hated—entire characters, subplots, decades—I realized that this particular story might work better as a novella. In fact, it might be perfect for that second Subterranean book. Gradually, the would-be fifth novel turned into the novella *Plastic Jesus.*

People love to ask writers where we get our ideas, but they don't seem to like it if the answer is too obvious. I've heard it said that my novel *Exquisite Corpse* is "nothing more than a blow-by-blow retelling of Jeffrey Dahmer's crimes." (Funny, I must have missed the news of Dahmer hooking up with another serial killer.) And Dahmer isn't even beloved by millions of people around the world.

I know there are a lot of Beatles nuts out there, and I figure a few of them will probably read this story, and some percentage of those will be pissed off by it. I can't help that. All I can say is that they are no more your Beatles than mine, and what I have created from the experience of listening to them is no less valid than the joy they've given you. If you just didn't like *Plastic Jesus,* fine, but I don't want to hear mutterings about how I have "desecrated" the Beatles' legacy. This idea is ridiculous for two reasons: (A) My story is a gnat compared to the herd of elephants that is the Beatles' legacy; (B) The Beatles always spoke out against prejudice, and if you think the homosexuality in this story desecrates their memory somehow, then your heart has been touched by something that they were never about.

I always get my ideas from the events and personalities of "real life." Some of these—the Lovecraft-like narrator of my story "His Mouth Will Taste of Wormwood;" Andrew Compton and Jay Byrne of *Exquisite Corpse;* Seth Grealy and Peyton Masters—remain recognizable through the veil of fiction. To those who consider this a failure of imagination, I confess that, by your definition, my entire body of work constitutes a failure of imagination; these are just the examples where you were able to recognize it. No, you can't get a refund, but if it bothers you, you can always stop buying my books.

To the rest of you—those who realize that *all* fiction is only "real life" twisted and reshaped by the mind of a writer—I offer no excuses; only the statement that, as with every other story I've published, I had no choice. I had to write it. I couldn't move on to anything else until I did. And it is finally the story I wanted to tell, and I have told it as well as I could.

＋━━❀━━＋

For information, unconditional love, and other things related to the writing and publication of *Plastic Jesus,* I'd like to thank Adam Alexander, Leslie Sternbergh Alexander, Marieke Bermon, Connie B. Brite, Ramsey and Jenny Campbell, Christopher DeBarr, David Ferguson (the Japan/acid/screaming scene was his idea and contains much of his language), Mary Fleener, Kaz, Linda Marotta, *Nerve* Magazine, William K. Schafer, Eddie Schoenfeld, Peter Straub, Richard Tuinstra, and Wolf. And a special thank-you to my agent, Richard Curtis, for understanding the form this story had to take, even though he might well have preferred it to become that elusive fifth novel.

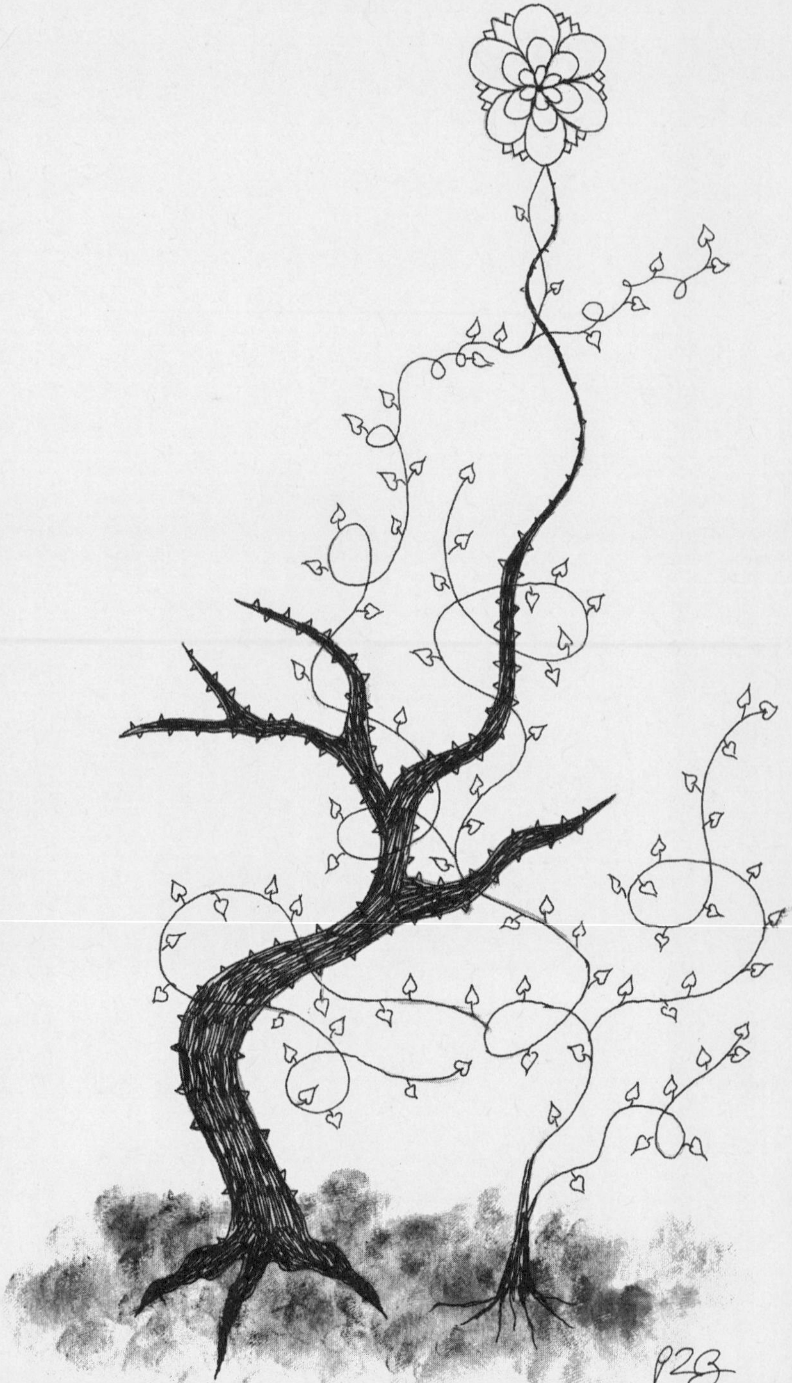